a

Everybody Feels...
SCARED!

Moira Butterfield & Holly Sterling

Eeeek!

Consultant: Cecilia Essau
Design: Barbi Sido, Mike Henson
Editor: Carly Madden
Editorial Director: Victoria Garrard
Art Director: Laura Roberts-Jensen
Associate Publisher: Maxime Boucknooghe
Publisher: Zeta Jones

First published in the UK in 2016 by
QED Publishing
Part of The Quarto Group
The Old Brewery
6 Blundell Street
London N7 9BH

www.qed-publishing.co.uk

A catalogue record for this book is
available from the British Library.

ISBN 978 1 78493 426 2

Printed in China

Contents

Feeling scared!

Everybody feels scared sometimes. You might get scared if...

...you have to do something in front of a lot of people.

...you have to go to a new place where you don't know anyone.

SCARED!

...you can't find your mum or your dad.

...you imagine that monsters and ghosts are real.

...you think something bad is going to happen.

How it feels

Your tummy is flipping
round and round.

Boom, boom!

Is that your heart?

Your legs feel wobbly.

You shake like jelly.

You must be...

Scared!

Scared boy

Hello. My name's Omar.
Last week **I** started a
new school.

OK.
Let's
go!

6

Before I went to school for the first time I felt really scared, and I didn't want to eat my breakfast.

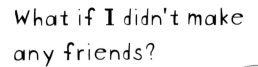

What if I didn't make any friends?

What if I went to the wrong classroom?

7

I walked to school really slowly. It felt as if my feet weren't working properly.

Being scared was no fun. It made everything feel hard to do.

Hi!

Then I met a girl called Chloe. She was in the same class as me.

She helped look after me, and showed me where to go.

This way!

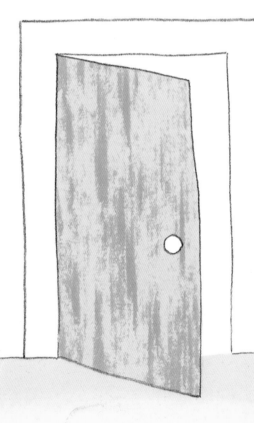

9

Then Chloe popped a little toy elephant in my pocket.
She said it was Beebee, her lucky toy.

You can borrow Beebee today, for good luck!

I felt better having Chloe for a friend, and having her lucky toy in my pocket.

In the end, I even forgot to feel scared!

Scared girl

Hello. I'm Chloe. Last week I found a huge shell at the beach, and my teacher asked me to bring it in for a show-and-tell lesson.

You can show us all tomorrow.

I thought about standing up in front of the whole class...
I thought about everybody staring at me.

I began to feel scared!

That night I couldn't sleep.

I kept thinking about having to stand up in front of everyone. It made my tummy feel all mixed-up inside.

14

I told my new friend Omar how I felt.

You will be GREAT!

He said that I shouldn't worry because my shell
was really beautiful and everybody would like it.

Then he reminded me that **I** could put Beebee
in my pocket to bring me good luck.

Thinking about Beebee in my pocket
helped me to feel less scared.

I was only a little nervous when I stood up at the front of the class.

Omar was right. Everybody liked my shell and I soon forgot to be scared.

Feeling better

With Chloe's help, Omar didn't feel
so scared on his first day at school.

With Omar's help, Chloe didn't feel so scared about standing up in front of the class.

They helped each other to do scary things and felt lots better when they went home.

Omar's story

1 Omar felt really scared before his first day at a new school.

2 Feeling scared made things hard to do, like eating breakfast and walking to school.

3 Omar's new friend Chloe helped him feel better on his first day. She even lent him her lucky toy.

4 He made more friends, and soon the scared feeling went away.

Chloe's story

1 Chloe was asked to stand up and talk in front of the class.

2 Thinking about it made her feel scared, and she couldn't sleep.

3 She told Omar how she felt and he made her feel less scared.

4 Her show-and-tell went well, and the scared feeling disappeared.

Story words

borrow
When you are given something, and give it back later. Omar borrowed Chloe's lucky toy elephant, Beebee.

flipping
When something is turning over and over. Your tummy might feel that way if you get scared.

heart
A part of your body that pumps your blood around. It works harder if you are scared. You might even hear it beating.

imagine
When you think of something that isn't real. You can imagine things that make you feel good or bad. It could be scary to imagine monsters and ghosts.

look after
To help someone and make sure they are OK. Chloe looked after Omar on his first day at school.

lucky
Something you think will help make good things happen. Chloe and Omar thought that Beebee was lucky, and that helped them both to feel better.

mixed-up

When things are mixed together, as if they were stirred around with a spoon. Chloe felt as if her tummy was all mixed-up inside.

nervous

When you feel a little bit scared of doing something. Chloe felt nervous standing up in front of lots of people.

properly

The way something should be done. Omar felt that his feet weren't working properly when he walked to school feeling scared.

show-and-tell

When children bring things into school to show their class. Chloe brought her shell into school.

staring

When somebody is looking at you for ages. Chloe was scared that everybody in class would stare at her when she stood up to talk.

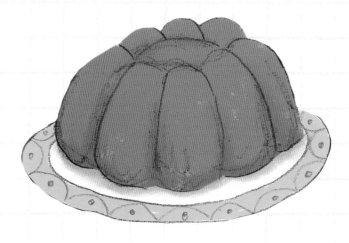

wobbly

When something shivers and shakes like a jelly. Feeling scared can make your legs wobble!

Next steps

These stories have been written to give children an introduction to feeling scared through events that they are familiar with. Here are some ideas to help you explore the feelings from the story together.

Talking

- Look at Omar and Chloe's stories. Talk about why they felt scared. How did it feel to be scared?

- Discuss how Chloe helped Omar to feel less scared. How did Omar help Chloe to feel better?
- Ask your child if they can remember a time when they felt scared, and why. Telling someone you know that you feel scared could be helpful – discuss how talking about their fear may help them feel better.
- Look at the poem on page 5 and talk to your child about how they feel when they are scared. You could help them write a poem themselves.

Make up a story

On pages 20–21 the stories have been broken down into four-stage sequences. Use this as a model to work together, making a simple sequence of events about somebody feeling scared and then feeling better. Ask your child to suggest the sequence of events and a way to resolve their story at the end.

An art session

Do a drawing session related to the feeling in this book. Here are some suggestions for drawings:

- A scared face, or somebody shaking like a wobbly jelly because they feel scared.
- Chloe feeling scared and not being able to go to sleep.
- Beebee, the little toy that helped Chloe and Omar feel reassured.

An acting session

Choose a scene and act it out, for example:

- Role-play Omar feeling scared as he goes to his new school. Act out him making friends with Chloe and borrowing Beebee. Then show him telling Chloe, or his mum if you prefer, how he feels less scared about being in his new school.
- Role-play Chloe feeling scared in bed about showing her shell at school. Role-play Omar helping her by reassuring her that she will be fine, and act out Chloe showing the class her shell and feeling better.